James Hickson

Early Poems

James Hickson

Early Poems

ISBN/EAN: 9783337158507

Printed in Europe, USA, Canada, Australia, Japan

Cover: Foto ©Andreas Hilbeck / pixelio.de

More available books at **www.hansebooks.com**

Early Poems:

BY

JAMES HICKSON.

———◆———

MANCHESTER:
SAMUEL M. STRONG, PRINTER, 84, MARKET STREET.
1872.

To

EDWARD HOLT, Esq.,

Cheetham, Manchester,

THIS WORK IS RESPECTFULLY DEDICATED, AS A MARK

OF GRATITUDE AND RESPECT,

FOR THE MANY FAVORS, BOTH FROM YOURSELF

AND YOUR HONOURED FATHER,

BY, DEAR SIR,

VERY GRATEFULLY YOURS,

THE AUTHOR.

PREFACE.

WHEN these Poems were originally written, the thought of them ever appearing in their present shape never entered the mind of the author. They are the simple, yet pure, outbursts of feeling which from time to time have exhibited themselves in my disposition, or nature ; and though many of my personal friends have advised me to turn my attention to something more profitable, yet I have not within myself either the will or power to expunge that gentle sensibility of feeling, which rises of its own creation, and warbles so sweetly into song.

A strong mind, by cultivation, may acquire, as it were, an art of writing poetry, but even in the best of all such efforts there will be seen a stiffness of style and a forced or unevenness of manner : whilst, on the contrary, should the verses from their own pure channel flow, we shall always have pleasure in their easy, flowing style, their sweetness of composition, their harmony of sound, and, withal, their force and vigour.

These things may not be acquired by learning, they are the natural gifts of nature ; hence the saying, "A poet must be born, not bred." The mind, says one of our great men, is man's standard ; and it may be as truly said, that man may be measured by the music of his soul. Hence there is a passion in the hearts of wise and virtuous people which leads them to read poetry with pleasure, because it endorses with truth those principles which they themselves, not only cultivate, but practise. Sadness, also, here finds its daily charm ; mirth, its companion in pleasure : and sorrow is dispelled by hope.

Therefore, believing these things myself, although my friends say poetry is a drug upon the market, I am inclined to take an opposite view of the question, and instead of printing only a small number of copies, I will issue what, if sold, will not only cover the cost of printing, &c., but will leave me a fair remuneration for my labour, which is also my delight. Let it, however, be clearly understood that the greater number of these poems were composed some years ago, and are not the productions of my present labours; but, being my early poems, I have carefully collected them together, and publish them in their present shape.

With these remarks, I trust my verses into the hands of my fellow-townsmen without any excuse or undignified lament, and thus I leave them, with the understanding that they are, as I have already said, my first and youthful efforts.

J. HICKSON.

April, 1872.

CONTENTS.

	PAGE
On a Birthday ...	9
Goodbye to Africa ...	13
What is Life ...	17
Lines to Mr. Peter Lea ...	21
A Mother's Care ...	25
Reproach Me Not Because I Sing...	29
They Say Thou Art a Flower as Fair ...	35
Persevere ...	39
Extract from Essay on Job ...	49
My Love Lives in a Fairy Dell ...	57
A Song ...	61
They Say Thou Art a Faded Flower ...	63
The Lifeboat ...	67

	PAGE
'Twas Night, and the Crested Billows Roll'd	73
Lines to My Canary	77
'Tis Autumn's Dawn	79
God Guard You	81
Lines Written in the Hour of Misfortune	83
Frown Not	85
A Dream and its Sequel	89
Town versus Country	107
Sad is My Heart	115
My God, and Can Thy Mercy Reach ...	117

ON A BIRTHDAY.

———

THIS happy greeting I have penn'd,
   Comes on your birthday from a friend,
Whose chief delight it is to send
               To Lizzie

The fond expressions of a heart
That loves its rapture to impart,
And warbles with poetic art,
               To Lizzie.

That she may bless this day that brings
Another birthday on its wings;
Calls happy memories back and sings,
               To Lizzie.

The songs of former days be thine,
Those songs so happy, so sublime,
That speak of love and truth divine,
                          To Lizzie.

And may each new born birthday find
These hopes still fresh within thy mind :
And Providence and friends be kind,
                          To Lizzie.

Then, as each birthday brings its close,
Thy mind will rest in sweet compose,
Till death shall bring a blest repose,
                          To Lizzie.

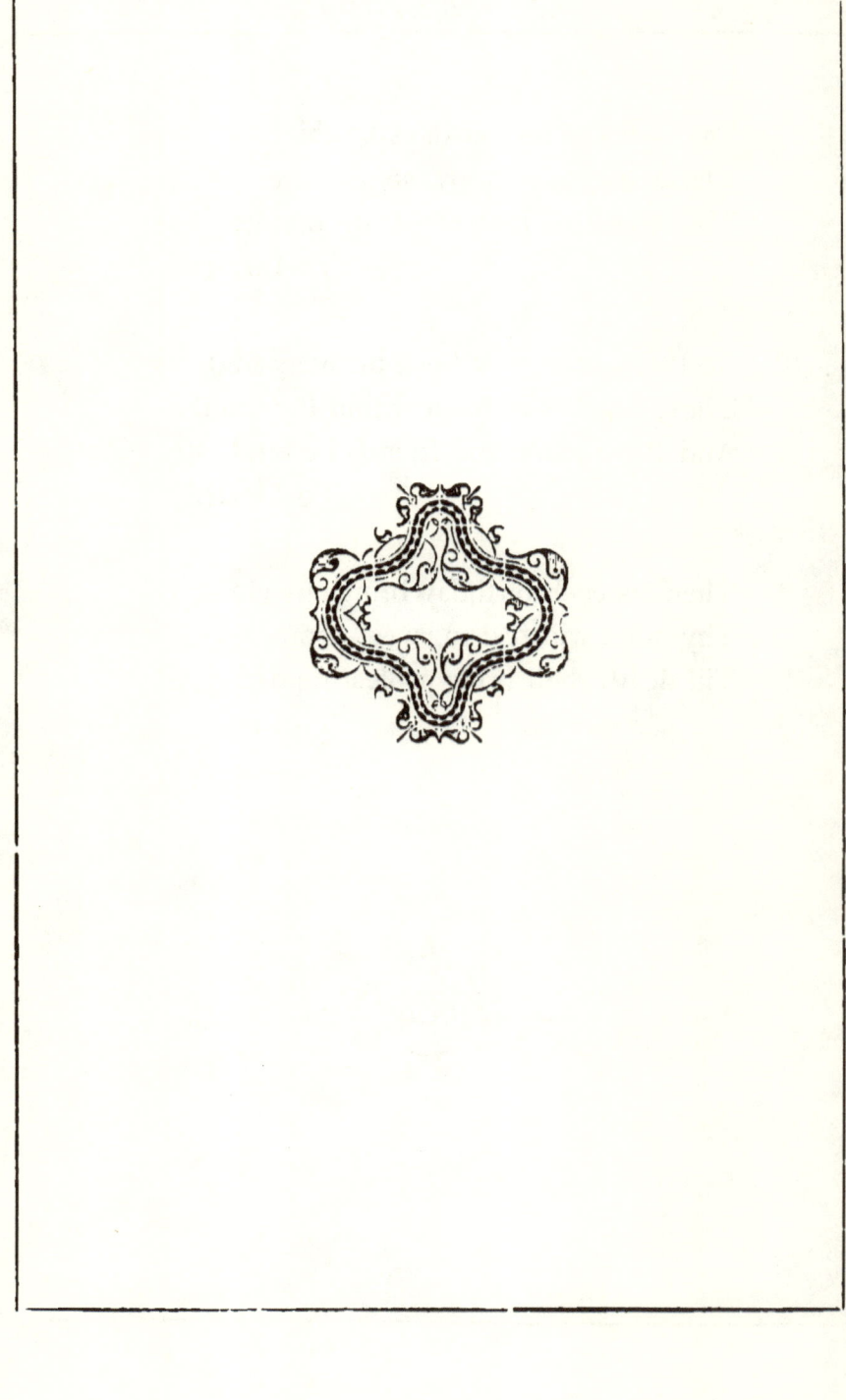

GOODBYE TO AFRICA.

G OODBYE to Afric's sunny shore,
    I look my last upon this plain :
Who knows if I may evermore
    Come back to thee again ?

A simple pledge to memory dear,
    I'll carry to my distant home ;
I'll give thee all I have—a tear,
    I'll take from thee—a stone.

And when, in future days to come,
    Though mighty seas between us roll.
I think upon what Britain's done,
    This pledge shall cheer my soul.

For once, from off this fertile shore,
    Thy sons were taken hence to toil :
Thy daughters, too, were basely bore,
    For purposes most vile.

But now the flag of England waves
    With all its pride against the breeze :
'Tis freedom's emblem to the slaves,
    'Tis master of the seas.

And proudly on thine own dear land
    The flag of Britain flouts the sky ;
And thousands of thy sons would stand
    Beside that flag and die.

At Cape Coast Castle, Sierre Leone,
    And very many places more,
They look to England as their home,
    Their monarch they adore.

Therefore I take this pledge from thee,
    I breathe my long, my last adieu :
The good thy sons have wished to me,
    I wish it back to you.

WHAT IS LIFE?

IT is not life, merely to live,
    To breathe the transient air :
Nor is it manly yet to give
    The heart up to despair.
For life it has a wider page,
    More noble, honest, true ;
And for a moment I'll engage
    To read that page to you.

So learn that it is only life
    To live in love of all ;
To soothe a sorrow, calm a strife,
    To nourish those who fall ;
To shed a blessing broadcast round
    The sick or widowed poor :
Nor let the pangs of hunger sound
    Relentless at your door.

Yes, life itself can only be
　　Translated into love.
It is the image all must see
　　In Him, who from above
Came down His blessings here to give,
　　That we might them enjoy ;
For 'tis not all of life to live,
　　Or all of death to die.

So come and learn the noble part,
　　That constitutes a life :
From honest virtue never start,
　　Nor ever build up strife :
Let honest hearts but make us glad,
　　In God rejoicing go.
The world would not be half so sad,
　　Were life, but love, below.

THESE LINES WERE PRESENTED TO

Mr. PETER LEA,

As a token of respect and sympathy towards him on the Death of his Wife.

TURN, gentle mourner, fondly turn,
  And hush the plaintive sigh ;
Leave now the unimpassioned urn,
  For God wills all must die.
The queenly dame, the valiant knight,
  The rich man and the poor,
All equal in our Father's sight,
  Nor could their wealth procure
One lingering moment of a span
'Twixt life or death in maid or man,
  For death is always sure.

The mouldering dust falls to decay,
   That smile so sweet has fled ;
The heart that glowed in health to-day,
   Alas ! to-day is dead.
Those lips that loved to soothe thy care—
   To charm thee with their sound :
The eye that sparkled soft and fair,
   The forehead white and round :
These, and a thousand graces too,
That meekly shone on all she knew,
   Must slumber in the ground.

Yet dry the eye—disdain the tear,
   God wills who first must part :
To make His mercy held more dear,
   As sunshine to the heart.
And, as beneath His chastening rod,
   We sink into the grave,
'Tis sweet to know our gracious God
   Chastises but to save.
For He is merciful and kind,
Forgiving sins, that all mankind
   May meet beyond the grave.

A MOTHER'S CARE.

I HAVE watched thee. my child, through the long
　　hours of night,
　And rested my head on thy pillow ;
I have welcomed most gladly the bright beam of light,
　That hangs up aloft o'er the billow.

I have kissed thy pale cheek when the bright burning
　　tear
　From my eyes were rapidly falling ;
And I've prayed to my God, whose presence is near,
　Who has kept thee alive this morning.

I have called thee by name, with endearments dear,
    With all that before was pleasing ;
And now my sad heart is o'erladen with fear,
    To think I've my darling been teasing.

But now rest, oh rest on in kind nature's repose,
    Thy slumbers more gently taking :
For I'll watch o'er thy bed when thy soft eyelids close,
    And I'll kiss thee, my love, when waking.

REPROACH ME NOT BECAUSE I SING.

REPROACH me not because I sing
  Of praises due to God ;
Whose love and mercy ever bring
  To this sad earth He trod
That peace of mind we only find
Where charity, and love combined,
  Show forth the man of God.

'Tis not for me to sing in praise
  Of warriors of old ;
Nor should I tune the lyre to ways
  That modern statesmen hold ;
'Tis true I may presume to cast
Some good example from the last,
  And truths not often told.

There, too, morality might find
   Some mind great beauties blend ;
To virtue nor to justice blind,
   A sympathetic friend.
Their praise to sing my muse should ring,
But still, it is a nobler thing
   To let our thoughts ascend.

Some sing of Wellington, and some
   Sing of Nelson's glory ;
And in a stream will others come,
   With love and youth in story.
But were my skill as my desire,
For evermore I'd tune the lyre
   To God's great glory.

Virtue and love have been a theme
   In every poet's song :
And lays of liberty I deem
   His duty to prolong.
In this he acts a worthy part,
But still there is a nobler art,
   And still a nobler song.

Combine whatever grace can give,
   Or virtue can command :
No human heart did ever live
   One half so great, so grand ;
Why, heaven itself cannot contain
The glorious presence of His reign,
   Or His angelic band.

Why, then, reproach me not because
   His praises form my song ;
A poet must obey the laws
   That to his God belong.
So, journeying on through life to death,
I hope to spend my latest breath
   In His seraphic song !

THEY SAY THOU ART A FLOWER AS FAIR.

THEY say thou art a flower as fair
    As nature can divine :
But I behold no beauty there
    I'd ever wish were mine.
Thy face and form might well become
    The presence of a queen ;
But inward grace alone may come
    Within the poet's theme.

It is the only gem, his soul
    The love song can inspire :
While virtue lives, or ages roll,
    That song will not expire.

'Tis not the face or form we find
　So beauteous to view :
For reason bade us search the mind,
　Where greater beauties grew.

Many a bud in nature's walk
　Seems lovely as the rose :
Do thou approach the tender stalk
　No fragrance from it flows.
Therefore, like thee, 'tis not a prize
　Our hearts can e'er adore :
For inward grace alone can rise
　Our hearts to love thee more.

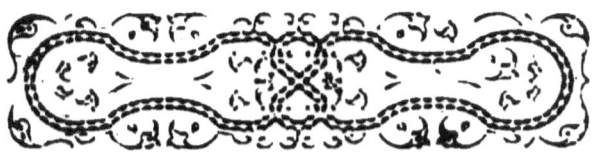

PERSEVERE.

The following lines were written with the view to inspire perseverance in all the honourable pursuits of life, particularly to the aspiring youth who may chance to read them. They will show him the value of selecting one course in life, and fixing then his determination to rise in that capacity. They will inspire him with courage to surmount difficulties, rise above calamity, and lead him with firmness to assail his task again and again : for it may be truly said that man creates for himself the greatest difficulties in the way of his own success.

A YOUTH of Britain's isle was seen.
   He was a comely youth I ween.
Boasting not of beauty ;
His greatest gift lay in his mind,
And that we presently shall find
   Bent alone on duty.

He had a home where love might dwell,
And pride might be content as well,
    But soon he left its shade :
And seeking out the path of fame,
To yon great hill he lately came,
    His resolution made.

Upon yon quiet spot he sat
And fixed his eyes on this and that,
    But nought seemed to dismay :
The spirit that within him ruled
Had evidently well been schooled
    To tread life's dangerous way.

He fixed his gaze at length on high—
The hill was buried in the sky,
    Its height was so extreme ;
But his sharp eye could pierce the gloom,
And now I saw a smile illume
    Where care before was seen.

I came and sat me by his side,
And would have learned his thoughts, and tried
    To move him from his plan :
But, " No," he said, " the way is clear,
I see a path right up from here
    Will reach the topmost span.

" Nor will I tread the way to fame
That other men have trod, who came
    To seal their future here ;
Yet here I'll risk, midst toil and strife,
My dearest hopes I have in life,
    The task my soul shall cheer.

" Upon yon hill I'll carve my name,
Nor idly sit and wish for fame :
    My soul cannot endure
The sluggish stream of every day,
That slowly bears one's life away.
    So homeless and so poor.

" Up, now, and doing, I ascend,
Nor own a friendly grasp, nor lend
    Idle thoughts on beauty ;
Friends would allure me from my way,
Or bid me try some other day,
    Keeping me from duty.

" I will not heed nor smiles, nor tears,
Nor men's disdain, or scoffs or jeers,
    Or love's glance inviting :
But proudly now I'll rush to fame,
And in his bosom seal my name,
    Life's great battle fighting."

'Twas thus he spoke, nor would he stay,
But like a torrent rushed away,
    Space increased behind him ;
He gave his motto to the wind,
'Twas wafted on the breeze behind,
    Nought could go before him.

O'er many a stream and gully's gash
He did with speed and safety dash,
    No glance behind was thrown :
'Twas onward, only onward still,
The task seemed easy, for the will
    Had man's great master grown.

But once or twice I saw him fall,
And thought he'd lost his life, his all,
    The danger was so great :
Again his form surprised my view,
Striving, struggling to pursue,
    He would for nothing wait.

He reached the peak, where twice he fell,
Assailed its point, and won it well :
    Then, lifting high his hand,
He shouted with a voice serene,
"My onward path is clearly seen,
    And easy to command."

One day the sun stood out on high,
And brightly lit the distant sky,
  Induced me here to stop ;
That youth with care my heart did fill,
I therefore sought him on the hill,
  And found he'd reached the top.

I waved my hand to him, and he
Exulting waved his hand to me,
  In youthful pride and joy :
'Twas then I understood the bard.
In life there nothing is too hard
  For man, if man will try.

And failing once, or even twice,
Let him assail the object thrice,
  Should honour point the way ;
And, in the end, he'll surely find
'Twas half accomplished when his mind
  Had lent its willing way.

Whatever task, my friend, be thine.
However thou wouldst wish to shine,
  Determine in thy mind :
Then be thou sure the prize to gain :
Yet honour's path's a path of pain,
  And that thoul't surely find.

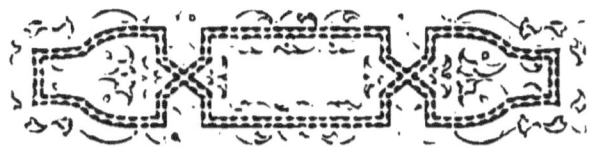

EXTRACT FROM ESSAY ON JOB.

The following lines are an extract from a poem that will form the subject of my next publication, but which is very much too long for insertion here. The author's object is to convey an idea of what the poem is likely to be.

The following lines occur after Job has been visited the second time by Satan's ministers of ill; the boils have broken out upon him, and he lies on the ground, &c. The argument is how little we think of sickness as we find ourselves recovering from it, and all the good thoughts of amending our lives are soon lost; then, the value of God's Holy Word, and also of Job's example.

BUT man seems ever to forget the strife
    That burned within him to consume his life :
The pain remitted, all his prospects seem
To flash upon the mind, as 'twere a dream.
Familiar faces, and delusive joys,
High hopes of fame, or lesser worldly ties,
With their allurements, steal the heart away
To quite forget the lesson of the day.
Hence the great blessing of that book divine,
Which every heart bears witness to be Thine,
Whose " still, small voice," when admonitions fail,
Can wake the reckless soul to mourn and wail,

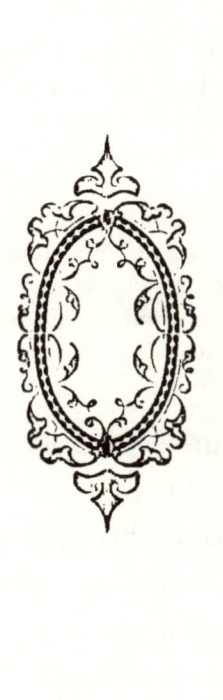

And flee from folly's dangerous estate
To paths of virtue that are truly great ;
And, in the transit, learn the written way
That guides the soul to everlasting day.
Therefore the profit were beyond compare,
Rich in its wisdom, wonderful and rare :
It opens wide a prospect for the poor
To purchase joys that ever shall endure :
It melts the heart by tender strokes of woe ;
Makes scalding tears in rivulets to flow ;
Then, as it doth the gracious work begin,
We reap the blessing, we despise the sin :
And, that this blessing may the more abound,
Within the book examples may be found,
Which show to every man his separate grief,
And breathes the antidote that gives relief.

For instance, what in cultivated art
Can near such moral excellence impart ?
Or what, in nature's powerful estate,
Can learn man in his sufferings to be great,
And hold a mirror up, that every age
Its war 'gainst Satan may with triumph wage ?
Where shall we turn for comfort and relief ?
Where shall we leave our heavy load of grief ?
'Tis not within the memory of man,
Or book or fable, since the world began,

To show us any other source where woe
Its grief dismantles, and pure comforts flow,
Save but the wisdom of the wondrous page
Whose mighty love can melt hell's cruel rage,
Satan disarms, makes evil visions fly,
Hides all our sorrows, and creates our joy.

Then, since such blessings 'tis thy power to give,
Oh ! let us ope the book and learn to live !
Yea, let us turn its pages o'er, and see,
Job, in thy miseries, how it worked on thee.
The mind can see thee suffering again,
Prostrate on earth, and agonized with pain,
Scraping thy sores with piece of potter's clay,
The ulcerous matter casting it away :
No friendly hand a kindly act to do ;
Bereft of children and of servants too :
A wife unkind ; too poor a sage to fee ;
Yet, robbed of all his joys, he turns to thee,
And finds a hope unspeakable with joy
Swell in his heart and whisper God is nigh.

Come, then, ye poor and lowly men of heart,
Drink of this blessing, bid your care depart,
To you is proffered what no wealth can buy,
A peaceful mind, a heart that's full of joy :
A happy journey o'er life's rugged shore,
Where those who sigh shall learn to sigh no more.

But bear the ills inherent with our life,
Calmly resigned to suffer in the strife ;
Yet fixed in hope eternity to find
More than a refuge for redeemed mankind !

Now these great mercies, counsellors of love,
Are rained upon the heart by God above ;
And hence it is, the good man's strange career
Is but an exercise of faith ; though fear
May for a passing moment cause a doubt
Whether his lamp of love is burning out ;
This but inflames a gentle frenzy still,
Lays bare the heart, and opens wide the will ;
Extracts a folly, singles out for foe
Some ruling passion that he must o'erthrow.
Thus waked at last to see his sinful state,
He also sees God's mercies must be great.
And in his gratitude of heart will bear,
Like Job, his troubles—rise above despair ;
For see him stretched upon the ashes now,
And mark the solid aspect of his brow :
No fickle change, nor no uncertain doubt,
He knows God's purpose must be carried out.
He gives his heart entirely up to Him,
Admits his fault, acknowledges his sin,
And praises God whose mercies, like the sun,
To endless ages shall for ever run.

MY LOVE LIVES IN A FAIRY DELL.

MY love lives in a fairy dell
   Surrounded by an upland lawn :
And there a crowd of lovers dwell
   At evening's gentle dawn.

And some are gay and rich and free,
   With ease and pleasure at command :
Yet midst them all not one like me
   Can press her gentle hand.

Yet I am poor, and daily toil
   To win from nature nature's bread ;
With care to cultivate the soil,
   Nor by ambition led.

I love her not for all the gear,
   For all the wealth she ere can own :
'Tis but her heart I prize and fear,
   For 'tis so like my own.

Oh, she is rich in nature's gifts,
    Her soul's immaculate, divine ;
Her worth inspires my heart and lifts
    My spirit up to Thine.

Yes, she is like the fairest dream
    Ere pictured by the power of love ;
Her grace would ornament a queen ;
    Her virtues shine above.

For she is pure in heart and mind,
    Her sympathies are always sure ;
And most compassionate and kind
    Alike to sick or poor.

And though these lovers proudly press,
    She knows their vows are empty guile ;
So none, with all his lordly dress,
    Can rob me of her smile.

A SONG.

I HAVE basked beneath the sunshine
   Of many a beauty's smile :
I have spent the merry May time
   In hours of artless guile :
But never, Liz, oh never.
   Did I such beauty see.
As in thy heart lives ever.
   And lives alone for me.
      Yes, 'twas thy heart, my Lizzie,
        And that loving smile of thine.
     That stole from me for ever
      A heart that's only thine.

Though I love that soft eye gazing
   With its sweet and modest hue :
Though I love thy bright hair waving.
   Thy form so graceful too :
Yet should these charms all fade thee,
   I'd still a beauty find,
For, more than all, I love thee
   For beauties of the mind.
      Yes, 'twas thy heart, my Lizzie,
        And that loving smile of thine,
     That stole from me for ever
      A heart that's only thine.

THEY SAY THOU ART A FADED FLOWER.

THEY say thou art a faded flower,
 Art false to love and me :
They say that heart feels not the power
 That mine doth feel for thee.

And is it true? ah, yes! that cold
 Disdainful smile doth show,
The love that was so sweet of old
 Has vanish'd long ago.

Yet, no! 'tis false— the power of love
 Unchangeable must be :
For though 'tis ever born above,
 Still it descends to thee.

And, placed where it delights to grow,
 How sweet its blossoms are :
For truth and innocence will go
 Beside it as a star.

Then, learn ! oh, learn ! that woman must
　To her first love be true :
For there she places all her trust,
　And all her prospects too.

Nay, more, and woman's heart doth know,
　The truth my verse will tell,—
That woman loves but once, I know,
　And loves her first love well.

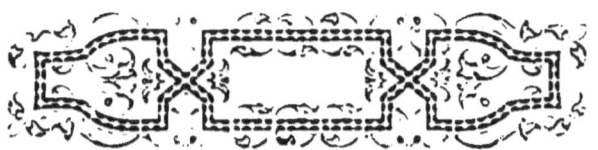

THE LIFEBOAT.

THE lifeboat skims the stormy sea,
    Floats on the angry main :
Is lost to sight, and now we see
    It drive before the gale.

Up ! up and down, yet wildly on,
    It skips from wave to wave,
As 'twere a feather, cast upon
    The wind to seek a grave.

Stout hearts, strong hands are at the oars,
    The boat glides swiftly on :
Far, far behind she leaves the shore,
    Yet still they urge her on.

On ! to what end ? we ment'lly ask,
    Why should she tempt the wave ?
For in this angry flood who bask
    Seek an immediate grave.

But hark ! a cry comes from afar ;
  Far o'er the surging sea :
'Twas loud enough almost to mar
  The waters vast and free.

It sounded dreadful in the night,
  As shriek on shriek arose :
For nature cried with all her might ;
  Then came a dull repose.

And then, oh joy ! a wilder cry
  Burs on the evening air :
'Twas answered by a hoarse reply ;
  Strong hearts and hands were there.

And then, as though by magic spell,
  The moon began to rise
From out black vapours, and she well
  Lit up the dismal skies.

Her pale reflection then was cast
  Upon the stormy sea :
A vessel, driven by the blast,
  Was all that one could see.

A fated vessel, for she sank
  Beneath the billows wild,
Nor left a firm or friendly plank
  To succour man or child.

The lifeboat still lives in the storm,
 Its mission is to save
Those creatures, helpless and forlorn,
 From an untimely grave.

And well she does her work ; thank God
 That there are men so brave,
To go where none but Christ e'er trod
 Successful on the wave.

All honour to those brave and bold,
 Those hearts so strong and free :
Well may their val'rous deeds be told,
 From age to infancy.

From age to infancy again
 So honoured be their shrine ;
Warriors then we'll think the men,
 Whose deeds are so sublime.

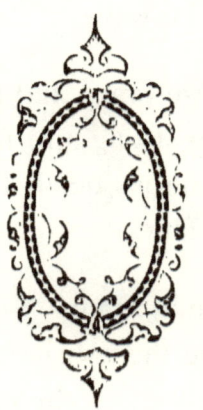

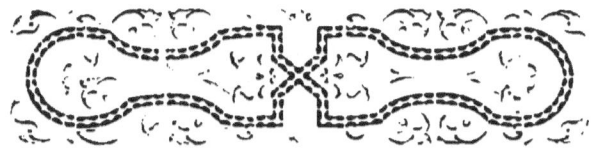

'TWAS NIGHT, AND THE CRESTED BILLOWS ROLL'D.

The following lines were composed on seeing a ship on fire at sea. She drifted ashore on the isle of Madeira. We afterwards learned she was the ironplated ship, "Elizabeth Flemming," and her passengers and crew had escaped in her boats.

'TWAS night, and the crested billows roll'd
    But slowly onward to the lee,
When a distant bell was loudly toll'd :
For we heard it plainly, as it roll'd,
    From eastward, o'er the sea.

It rang an alarm. We scan the sky ;
    Madeira's wrapt in midnight gloom ;
We look to the east, south-east, and cry,
For a volley of flames had lit the sky,
    And a vessel had met its doom !

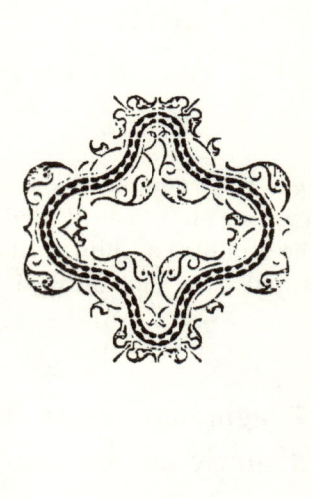

Our skipper calls, with a hoarse command :
    " Aye, aye !" is the seaman's reply ;
" Hard-a-starboard, boy, and pipe all hands,
Our help yon ship and her crew demands,—
    We'll give it, lads, with joy !

" Take in all sail bear up to the wind--
    Now, steady," is the captain's command :
" Run out your starboard gun there, and mind
A message ye send yon ship, designed
    To prove a friend's at hand !"

We neared the ship on her larboard bow,
    All her masts by the board had gone ;
Enveloped in fire—above, below,—
Her plates were bright with a burning glow :
    Her planks and spars were gone.

No one could live on that burning deck !
    What, then, had become of her crew ?
Say, had they wisely escaped the wreck
When all in their means had failed to check
    The flames that round them flew.

For not a soul on that wreck appear'd :
    And, though the flames had lit the sky,
No boat was seen, as the wreck we near'd,
So our hopes were lost—her crew, we fear'd,
    Had left her but to die.

LINES TO MY CANARY.

NO bird that sings in Eastern skies,
  Or any other spot that lies
    Betwixt the poles and me,
Sings not with notes more blythe or gay,
The sweet the happy hours away,
    My little bird, than thee.

Although but nine or ten months old,
Much melody thou dost unfold
    To an attentive ear;
Thine's not the music taught by art,
'Tis nature speaks in every part,
    For nature's hand is here.

No sadness ever comes from thee,
Thy notes are always soft and free,
    So very sharp and clear:
They seem to raise within my mind
Some happy feeling of the kind
    That makes thy music dear.

'TIS AUTUMN'S DAWN.

FAREWELL! Farewell! 'tis Autumn's dawn,
 And we must lose for ever
The rose that bloomed beside the thorn,
 And charmed so well together.

Tho' we have loved their golden hue,
 And breathed their fragrant sigh,
Nature now proclaims her due,
 And every flower must die.

Their dress so lovely, so serene,
 Is no protection now ;
Their brightest blush may die unseen,
 Or wither on the bough.

Just so will Autumn dawn in life,
 Nor can the brilliant flower
Bloom at the close of Autumn's strife,
 Or live in Winter's hour.

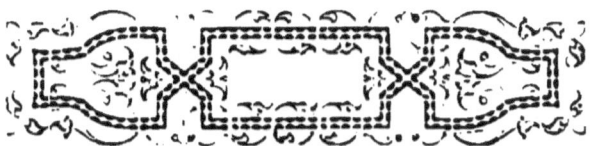

GOD GUARD YOU.

FROM every danger, every care,
From every thing that brings despair.
From every sin that follies share.
    God guard you.

From every care the heart can feel.
From every slander tongues reveal.
From every thing that works not weal.
    God guard you.

From every danger of the waves.
From every sin that makes us slaves.
From all that makes us fear our graves.
    God guard you.

From all that keeps you from His love.
From all that makes you fear the dove.
And whispers there's no heaven above.
    God guard you.

LINES WRITTEN IN THE HOUR OF MISFORTUNE.

GREAT God, preserver of my life,
  In whom all comforts shine,
Be pleased to still the angry strife
  In this sad heart of mine.

Extend Thy gracious hand, to save
  This heart so faint with care,
That lives upon the world's cold wave
  A friendless, homeless fare.

Thy punishments are just, I know,
  My heart speaks they are true :
But all Thy vengeance, God, forego,
  Forgive Thy servant too.

And teach me in this world to prize
  The gifts Thy hands bestow,
And let Thy counsels make me wise,
  In paths of peace below.

FROWN NOT.

FROWN not, should providence refuse to smile
   On some unhappy, some misguided man,
Who from the point of honour once could rile
   On meaner nature, still design'd as man.

Forgive him, if the love of worldly wealth
   Had for a time defaced his nobler part :
Nor let the indignation of thyself
   Create a living monster in thy heart.

Glut not thyself with pride because he fell
   As much beneath thee as he once was more :
Perhaps the wheel of fortune--who can tell—
   May soon descend upon thy gilded store.

For know, the ways of providence and God
   Are both identical, are both the same,
And here with wisdom He doth use the rod,
   And there it pleaseth Him to scatter fame.

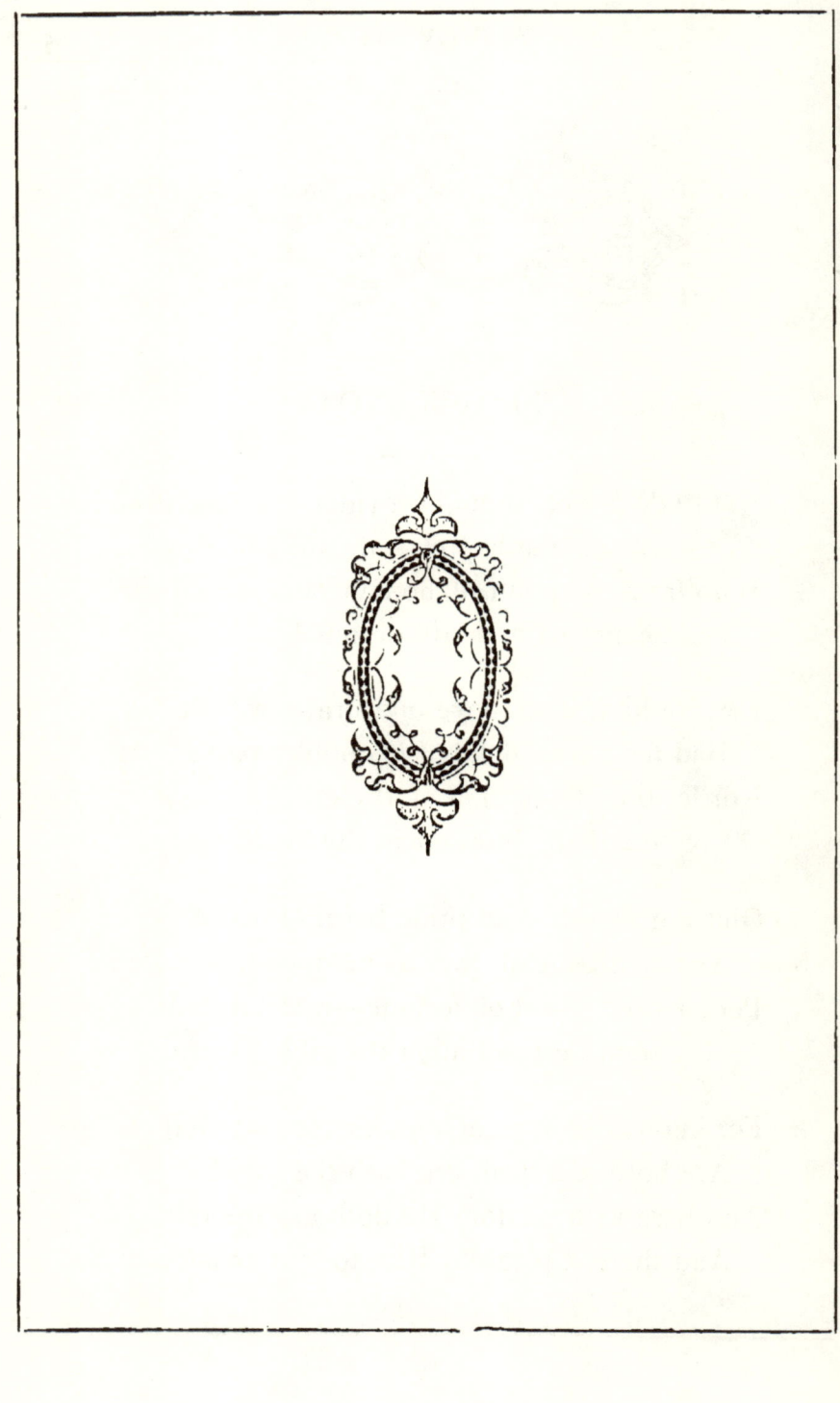

Then, be not thou presumptuous to scan
    The earthly policy of Him who reigns
As well o'er principalities as man ;
    O'er seas and oceans, deserts, mountains, plains.

Then go not with the ignorant, or frown
    Upon the man thou once esteemed a foe :
'Tis far more noble, when thou seest him down,
    To give thy charity and let him go.

A DREAM AND ITS SEQUEL.

———

A MILE from the spot where I sit,
   Lived a man of whom I shall tell :
He rejoiced in the surname of Pitt.
   Though some called him Billy as well.
Now this story of Billy's 'tis true,
   Though some won't believe what I say ;
But I'll now relate it unto you,
   As it was related to-day.

Billy lived in a street off Shudehill,
   His house, up a court, in a lane ;
And if he had been living there still,
   Why still he had lived in the same.
Now this man he was fond of a glass,
   And, had he a copper or two,
Then the nearest tavern to pass
   Was more than poor Billy could do.

Now the twelve sterling hours of a day
    Would pass him with care or delight :
But this Billy would drink, so they say,
    Half way through the shadows of night.
Then at three in the morning, or so,
    With many a stagger and skip,
Right away up Shudehill he would go
    Each moment expecting to slip.

He could find his house well in the dark,
    Preferred going home in the gloom :
For he used to account it a lark
    To go by the light of the moon.
Now his door would be left at his will
    To open or shut as he chose :
Yet within 'twas so deathly and still,
    He said that it gave him the blues.

'Twas on such an occasion, they say,
    One morn Billy went to his bed,
And lay there, oh, so late the next day
    That every one thought he was dead.
But poor Billy awoke with a shout,
    A scream too terrific to tell,
As he glared with his eyes all about,
    And shouted he'd come back from hell.

Then he yelled with his might and his main :
    He gnashed in his fury and spleen :
All his frame seemed to writhe in his pain,
    Till convinced 'twas all but a dream.

Even then he was sorely afraid,
  As he lay on his back in bed :
"Oh ! come round me, and listen," he said,
  "While I tell my story so dread."

Now his wife and his children and friends,
  Come round, all impatient to hear :
And as patiently wait, till he ends
  His tale so amazingly queer.
" I have had such a dream," he began.
  "'Tis almost too dreadful to tell :
For I dreamt that, one night as I ran
  Upstairs, I fell down into hell.

" Yes, I'd almost ascended the stairs—
  Quite drunk at the time, I must own—
When as backwards, midst tables and chairs,
  I fell with a terrible groan.
I had broken my neck in the fall,
  And took an immediate flight
Through a passage, dark, dreary, and small,
  I came to an heaven of light.

" And this was quite a large, spacious room,
  Unlimited, far in extent.
And was such a relief from the gloom,
  That towards it my footsteps I bent.
It was lit with a strange looking light,
  That seemed to revolve in the air.
Just as though there was nothing but night
  E'er knew an inhabitant there.

" Every seat was quite full, and a crowd,
    Too many to number, stood by :
And each face seemed engulphed in a cloud,
    As though it knew nothing of joy.
Still the noise of the gamesters rang high —
    For each kind of gambling was there—
Yet the winners ne'er seemed but to sigh,
    The losers to howl in despair.

" Many clusters of men hung about,
    With glasses and pipes short or long ;
And some there were describing a rout ;
    Some here were admiring a song ;
Here and there some were speaking aloud ;
    And others, in whispers, would tell
Oh ! how heavy to bear was the cloud
    That hung on their spirits in hell.

" To a group of this kind I came near,
    They welcomed me all as I came :
' A new comer,' said one, ' it is clear,'
    They all iterated the same.
' Have a drink,' cried a man in a coat
    Full-buttoned, and down to his knee.
' Have a drink, cried they all, ' and devote
    Eternity now to a spree.'

" Here thou canst have thy greatest desire ;
    Thou canst drink, but never be full :
Drink only adds strength to the fire
    It never had ~~strength~~ power to annul.

Have a smoke, too, and join in a game,
  Whatever on earth was thy will,
Come, fulfil it, for here the same
  Desolation will haunt thee still.

" So, whatever thy pleasure has been,
  Whatever thy fancied delight,
Here to greatest perfection is seen
  In colours most glowing and bright.
So, indulge as you like, hope has fled,
  Joy, pleasure, and love dwell not here :
The bright visions of hope are all dead,
  And anguish is cradled in fear.

" Now, look round thee on every hand,
  Survey all this wonderful crowd :
Everyone did inhabit a land,
  And heard of salvation's sweet sound :
But we scoffed then at words of advice,
  We hated advisers of good :
And we doubted the truth beyond price,
  Nor believed in the Saviour's blood.

" Now redemption for us there is none,
  Contentment can never live here :
E'en the smallest of pleasure is gone,
  And comforts can never appear.
And, alas ! our great punishment see :
  Each heart is surrounded by fire,
So it will for eternity be,
  This flame it must never expire."

Saying this, he unbuttoned his coat,
　　Exposing his breast to my view ;
When the flames they flew up to his throat,
　　His heart they enveloped too !
I dropt both my pipe and my glass,
　　And instantly made for the door :
But, behold, there was no way to pass,
　　A gate had sprung up from the floor.

So, quite wild with despair, I began
　　To curse this unfortunate day ;
When close by my side a dreadful man
Who Grinned in a most horrible way.
　　" Nay, curse thou not," he cried, " it is vain ;
　　Yet curse if thou wilt, for, 'tis clear
Cursing and drinking have been the bane,
　　My friend, that has brought thee here.

" E'en on the earth thou hast lately trod,
　　My name all the clergy abuse :
Yet each may justly say to his God,
　　That cursing I never did use.
'Tis a mean and a cowardly act,
　　'Tis the most debasing of sin ;
I never was heard or caught in the fact,
　　Could never find profit therein.

" But now, come, thou must enter with me,
　　A place unto thee I'll assign,
Which for endless of ages shall be
　　Undoubted possession of thine."

As he spake I recoiled from his grasp,
   And begged he would let me depart ;
But my hand at that word he did clasp,
   And sent quite a thrill to my heart.

" Well, if thou wouldst go back," he replied,
   " Go, now I will open the way :
But just mind to be back,"—and he sighed
   Twelve months from this hour and this day.
For thy fate it is sealed, thou art mine :
   Return to thy friends for a year,
On the last stroke or second of time,
   Remember, my man, thou art here."

After this, on the instant I flew
   From hell, and returned to my bed.
And now, I have related to you
   My story so painful, so dread.
Oh ! thank God it's a dream, and from this
   Ne'er more a poor drunkard I'll be.
Come wife, and seal my pledge with a kiss,
   And in future I'll love but thee.

Now, for seven long months, I've been told,
   He looked not at a tavern he字 past,
Till the dream in his mind growing old,
   He broke his resolve at the last ;
And twelve months from the day of his dream,
   As Billy was going to bed,
Falling down all the stairs, it would seem,
   Had broken his neck, and was dead.

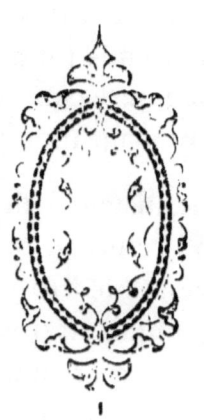

Moral, or Conclusion.

My story thus ends : 'tis not ours to know,
  As yet, the sequel to this dream so true :
But those who scoff at Providence may show
  There is no lesson here for me nor you.

Oh, be advised, persuaded by the book,
  These dreams and visions are not all a blank :
Into their purport take a prayerful look,
  And give them credence as they seem to rank.

In ancient days, when time itself was young,
  The honoured fathers of the Hebrew race,
Of dreams and visions they have sweetly sung,
  And given each in prophecy a place.

Therefore, since God has made these dreams to be
  Sometimes a channel for prophetic sight,
Jest not at visions that are sent to thee,
  God often shows his mercy in the night.

What child ere grew to manhood's firm estate,
  Though smooth or rugged as his lot might seem,
Without the knowledge of a something great
  Foreshadowed in the shadow of a dream ?

How many ills have been averted by,
  And so-called accidents prefixed before,
How many warnings of the death they die
  Could form the subject of prophetic lore.

Then be thou wise in this dissembling age,
    Think of the warnings thou hast had before ;
They speak aloud, do thou but mark the page,
    Turn from thy folly, then, and sin no more.

Should heaven be pleased to warn thee of a foe,
    Or show the danger of a coming day,
Put thou thy trust in Providence, and go
    Calmly rejoicing o'er the dangerous way.

Prepare thy heart whene'er presentments come,
    The foretold evil lags not far behind ;
Repair the harm, if thou hast any done,
    And even to an enemy be kind.

Nor think that fate is but an empty sound,
    There's some divinity thy end will shape ;
Try, try the heart, for there the sequel's found,
    And be thou just, and generous, and great.

TOWN VERSUS COUNTRY.

NOW sinks the sun's decaying stroke,
    Soft. tender moonbeams kiss the sky
And night is scaling with its cloak
    What charms the wearied eye.

My soul surveys this scene of bliss,
    And wonders at its calm repose ;
To think a day in life like this
    Could so serenely close.

All, all is hushed beneath thy glow,
    Pale majesty and star of heaven ;
Couldst thou but still man's bosom so,
    And calm what God has given.

Alike in thee the will or power,
　Thou harbinger of night's approach ;
Thy movements indicate the hour
　Satanic deeds encroach.

Now runs the city high with glee,
　Half hid beneath thy dusky cloak ;
And vice of every degree
　God's providence provoke.

For thieves and base assassins steal
　Securely forth beneath thy shade,
To drive against the public weal
　A vile and drunken trade.

A thousand hearts a thousand ways
　Debasing roads of ruin tread ;
Yet 'cause calamity delays,
　Calamity's not dead.

Oh, no ! the subtle foe's at hand,
　We surely reap that we do sow ;
The labour of the heart, the hand
　Is partly paid below.

I turn from this, and look with love
　Upon yon smiling, healthy plain ;
All, all directs the heart above,
　And fain would still its pain.

For more than sweet at evening's close,
  A scene like this so lovely fair :
To breathe the fragrance of the rose
  That's wafted on the air.

Here in many a lovely dell,
  Many a shady lane like this,
The swain his song of love will tell,
  And steal the parting kiss.

And now, from toil in wood or moor,
  The honest workman bends his way
To where he feels himself secure
  Against the storms of day.

His children run to meet him, when
  They hear his hand upon the door :
And kiss and kiss him o'er again,
  Yet ask for one kiss more.

The wife—his home with studied care,
  In every part so neat and clean
Draws forth the comfortable chair,
  Contented as a queen.

Though frugal their repast may be
  Health wants not sauce or dainties there ;
He takes his wife upon his knee—
  He hears his children's prayer.

He feels himself a man whom God
  Exalted ever with his love ;
He's bravely tried and fairly trod
  The way for home above.

His children neither hear nor see
  The vice great cities ever share ;
Life's page with them must surely be—
  To meet thy God prepare.

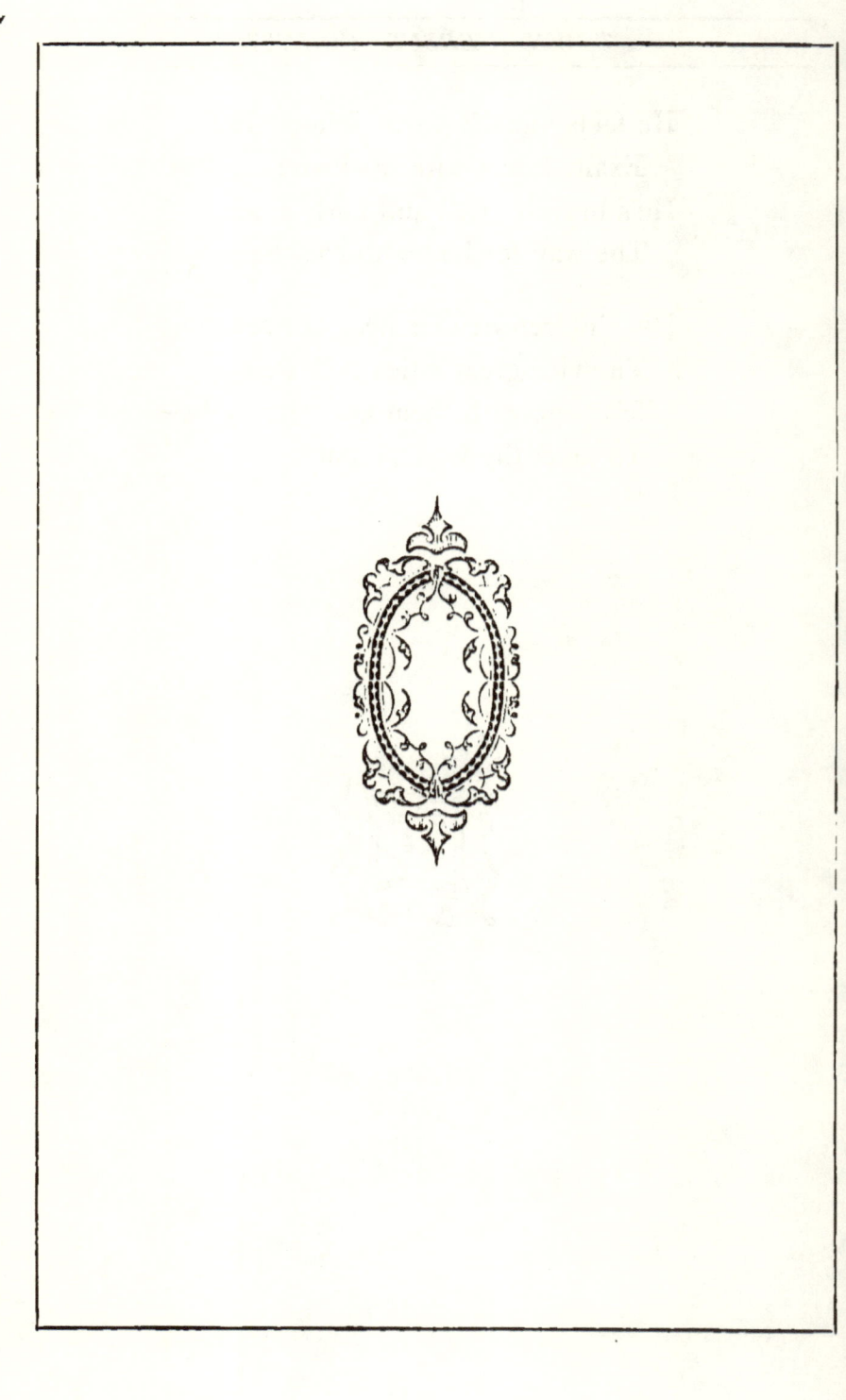

SAD IS MY HEART.

SAD is my heart when memory dwells
　　On scenes that have gladdened before ;
My bosom with anguish rapidly swells
　　As I count all my evils o'er.
I mourn in my heart, yet my lips convey
　　No sound that the world can hear :
'Tis the silent prayer of a soul's dismay,
　　It rises with many a tear.

In trespass and sin lies my heart now dead,
　　'Tis more than a stranger from God ;
Yet more I think, I diminish the dread
　　He brings with His chastening rod.
Tenacious my mind of many a fault,
　　Yet some things are equally clear :
'Tis Christ's tender mercy to blind, lame, halt—
　　Yes ! these make His memory dear.

Then let me think of His promise again,
　　His gracious forgiveness explore ;
Learn from His book how His mercy to gain,
　　And evil transgressions deplore.
Return to thy peace, my soul, and be blest,
　　Oh ! accept of thy Saviour's love ;
I learn that He died, to bring thee to rest
　　In kingdoms of peace up above.

MY GOD, AND CAN THY MERCY REACH.

MY God, and can Thy mercy reach
    A sinful soul like mine ;
May I believe the word they preach,
Those ministers who say they teach
    That blessed word of Thine.

Oh ! can Thy love for sinful man
    Avert Thy justice now ;
They say that since the world began
Thy word has very swiftly ran,
    And hearts before Thee bow.

Yet how can this affect my cause,
    Thine anger from me turn ;
Or hide me from the many flaws
Inflicted 'gainst Thy holy law,
    That Satan bade me spurn.

Can human heart, or man's great mind,
    Advance some signal way :
Will cleanse me from the guilt I find
That doth my soul to torture bind,
    That dooms me to dismay.

Ah no, alas! no heart is true,
  No soul is righteous, none ;
From heaven did God creation view,
To find but one His will to do,
  Alas! He found not one.

Yet not, alas! the more should we
  Our loud hosannas sing :
For God allowed His Son to be
A sacrificial Lamb for me
  A great redeeming King.

And by His blood so freely shed
  On Calvary's great cross :
And by His rising from the dead,
He's pacified my God, and led
  Me homeward without loss.

For whosoever shall believe
  In Christ shall never die ;
And though our sins should make us grieve,
God's truth our hearts will not deceive,
  Nor can the Father lie.

Oh, then my soul, awake, and give
  Thy sweetest song to Him :
Whose pleasure it has been to live
Here upon earth, and here to give
  His life to hide thy sin.

www.ingramcontent.com/pod-product-compliance
Lightning Source LLC
Chambersburg PA
CBHW032019010726
47493CB00007B/2476